CONE
Transformed

C O N E
Transformed

Twenty-One Episodes
from the Remarkable Life
of Doctor Ephrastus Cone
Medieval Metaphysician
& Conjuror

as recorded by

Bob Heman

POETS WEAR PRADA • Hoboken, New Jersey

Cone Transformed

Poets Wear Prada
533 Bloomfield Street, Second Floor
Hoboken, New Jersey 07030
http://pwpbooks.blogspot.com

First North American Publication 2021
First Mass Market Paperback Edition 2021

Grateful acknowledgment is made to the following publications where some of the episodes first appeared: *Artful Dodge*, *Skidrow Penthouse*, and *White Rabbit*. The first twelve episodes were previously collected in the chapbook titled *Cone Investigates*, and the final nine in a private edition titled *Cone Unearthed*.

ISBN-13: 978-1-946116-22-2   ISBN-10: 194611622X

Printed in the U.S.A.

Collages: Bob Heman
Author Photo: Ed Barnas

For my cousin
E d G o o d w i n
whose early example and encouragement
helped me set out on my journey
through the forest of words

Table of Contents

CONE
Transformed

CONE TRAVELS

Dr. Cone is tied into a metal frame and lowered over the edge of the map. Rapidly he leaves the world of concepts behind, plunging instead into a land of forces and junctures. They do not see him at all in this new land. He is felt the way a dream is felt, gone before they can even be sure what he was. The journey remains incomprehensible to him, memorable at points only because of the state his mind was in when he reached them. The details are not there at all, almost as if he had read about it in a book. And perhaps he had. The map and arrows seem to lead him only in circles, back ever again to the edge where the rivers start, cut irrevocably like the slice of the knife that sends the lucky ones back again and again from the altar to sit with the gods.

CONE INVESTIGATES

Dr. Cone herds a dozen or so of his clones down a dirt road deep into the forest. He is taking them to a distant clearing where he hopes they will aid him in his research. The clones, though, have a tough time staying on the path, having a tendency to wander off in all directions. Eventually they reach the clearing. There the doctor positions them around himself, but the minute he goes back to his ancient tome they start to wander off again. By the time he begins his invocations over half of them have disappeared. He is able to control the rest more easily. Soon the preliminaries are finished. Just as he is about to initiate the special movement a scream is heard in the distance. Reluctantly he goes to find its cause. Three of the clones have cut open a wolf and are pulling out the partially digested body of a young girl dressed in red. Somehow she is still alive and keeps asking for her grandma. Dr. Cone does the only thing he can and puts the girl painlessly out of her misery. The hunter who has emerged slack-jawed from the thickets behind them lets out a surprised sigh. Once again they have given him the wrong script.

CONE TRANSFORMED

Dr. Cone visits the land of the hedonists. They view him as a cactus and try to avoid getting pricked. He sees only slippery mirrors and black velvet bags. The point at which he coincides with the mirrors is the point at which the hedonists think they have won. They remove his thorns as painfully as possible and make him enjoy every yank. They enjoy it too and give him a new name. He crosses the flood many times before they finally drop him into a different room. There he sinks rapidly out of sight. Before they can understand what has happened he is gone without a trace. When he opens his eyes he finds himself in the land of the puritans. They view him as a slimy mirror and start the game all over again.

CONE WRITES

Dr. Cone has written a truly endless book. It is an accordion book that unfolds and unfolds and unfolds out of its little box and tells the story of a man whose duty it is to open doors. Each door he opens reveals another door and then another and another as the book continues to be pulled from its little box, telling the story of the man who opens doors, the man who wishes that just one of them, sometime, would be locked.

CONE DREAMS

The Wise Men nail the infant Jesus to the cross. They have the gift of foresight and understand that all things are inevitable. They send shepherds to visit the baby Judas with thirty pieces of silver. An innkeeper is dispatched to find the toddler John the Baptist and to bring back his head, which is then sent to the baby Salome with a somewhat incoherent note. The young Pontius Pilate is taught, after killing a neighbor's cat, how to wash his hands of the whole affair. With some difficulty two young thieves, not yet versed in their father's trade, are also found and crucified. Only the delinquent Barabbas cannot be located. He is out of town and no one knows when he will return. The doctor searches for him in the neighboring villages, entering each house to question the startled inhabitants. The rooster crows just as he reaches the door that he is sure is the right one.

CONE AWAKENS

Dr. Cone awakens from an unusual dream and goes out to buy a new rooster. The old one no longer crows at the proper time. Perhaps it has grown too old. Both its hearing and eyesight are failing. The hens no longer search for it and there have been no new chicks for a long time. The man in the market tells him that they no longer stock roosters and offers him a mechanical alarm instead. But he shakes his head sadly and goes back instead to his favorite clearing in the woods, where the rabbits all emerge from their damp burrows to look at him. He takes the fattest one and offers it, with the proper ancient words, as a sacrifice to the goddess of the dawn. Afterwards the first light always arrives an hour later so that the doctor can get his full night's sleep. The rooster too seems to benefit from the change. Soon little chicks are seen hurrying all around the yard.

CONE PAINTS

Dr. Cone thinks that he is the reincarnation of an ancient snowstorm. His fingers grow inexplicably numb even in July and the only color he ever fully sees is white. He is able to differentiate all of its three thousand four hundred and eighty-two known shades. He decides to become an artist and paints a series of variations on the color white. Since the art critics are not able to differentiate among the different shades, they applaud him for his courage in filling the grand gallery with five hundred and eighty-two blank white canvases. Through this misunderstanding Dr. Cone establishes his reputation in the field of art. He never paints another canvas. In this way his immortality is assured.

CONE PERFORMS

Dr. Cone pulls magic out of the rabbit and stuffs it into his hat. His assistant cuts the saw in half and throws herself around the knives. The stage is levitated over an unconscious volunteer. After the cabinet disappears into the doctor, coins begin to crawl back into his assistant's ear, and everywhere little paper flowers reappear to swallow up the doves. The doctor and his assistant continue to applaud even after the audience has gone.

CONE SHAVED

The wind gets trapped in Dr. Cone's beard and he does not know how to get it out. Around and around it swirls, knocking all the bats and owls from their resting places. It sings the song that the wind has always sung, alternately lulling the doctor into a semi-sleep and rousing him into fits of nervous fear. He can no longer think in his usual ways. In a moment of brief clarity he sends the hunchback to fetch the town smith who also serves as the local barber. When the smith arrives he finds the doctor in a trance-like state, his huge beard pulsing with a life of its own. The assistant relays the doctor's instructions, then disappears into the catacombs to leave the smith to do his work. He quickly has the doctor's face covered with a thick lather, even as the beard continues its palpitations. Soon tiny bubbles start to form along its edges. The smith opens his razor and strops it to a glistening sharpness. Then he begins. Carefully he makes his long strokes, again and again pulling the razor down the doctor's cheeks and along the edge of his chin. But something is terribly wrong. He lets out a sudden cry and drops the razor. Instead of the doctor's pale skin there is only a dark and unwholesome tunnel where the last of the bats quickly disappear from the sudden implosion of light. Deep in its recesses the wind continues its ancient and troubling song.

CONE DIES

Dr. Cone has died. All the creatures in the woods creep slowly up to his body and stare. When enough of them have gathered they sing the old song and watch as the doctor's body starts to rise back up into the air from which it had originally descended. The animals keep watching until it disappears behind some clouds. What they don't see is the scaly demon that unbuttons the doctor's chest from the inside and emerges holding in its teeth the bloody thing the doctor would have called his heart. The demon laughs for a while, then swallows the heart and walks away on the strangely textured air, turning back once or twice to watch the doctor's now empty skin floating silently back to earth. Later a farmer, pausing in his cabbage fields, recognizes at once the costume he finds lying between the rows. He wears it to the Halloween party at the farmer's club where he meets a lady in a strangely glowing dress who takes him back to her trailer. At an intensely sexual moment the farmer is struck from behind by a smiling hunchback who skins him of his costume, then exits quickly, leaving the lady to her promised and somewhat messy feast. The hunchback carries the skin back to the familiar clearing in the forest, where he stuffs it full of rocks and positions it in a sitting position. Soon all the little creatures are staring at it once again. They marvel at how the lumpy Dr. Cone has returned from the other place to silently guide them in their secret lives. As expected, the once wordy doctor is never again heard to utter another word. He becomes the best teacher they have ever known.

CONE CALCULATES

Dr. Cone visits the city of numbers. He slides inside of a seven and disappears for hours. When he is next seen everyone asks where he has been. He retracts his humanity until they disappear once again into the boiling ground. Then he lifts the lid that covers the place where the numbers grow. Into its thought soup he pours his own numbing hesitancies. In this way fractions are born.

CONE MELTS

Dr. Cone melts in the rain. He had always expected something like this would happen. His assistant tries to scoop him up in a crumpled paper cup, but it is too late. Down into the sewers he goes. Eventually he reaches the sea. He can only vaguely sense what was once his essence, now spreading rapidly in all directions. Soon he is no longer aware of anything at all. Meanwhile his assistant has dragged his bad leg down to the constable's office, but they are reluctant to do anything. No, no, they say, patting his hump a bit too familiarly, evaporating the sea is quite out of the question. Our science just hasn't progressed that far, and besides, even if it was possible, how would we find what is left. He must be scattered over hundreds of miles by now. No, it is simply out of the question. And so they lead the assistant back to the door and point him to the cathedral, where, they say, perhaps a few prayers wouldn't hurt. After all, you just never know.

CONE MARTYRED

Dr. Cone is stoned to death. His body is carried outside of the city to the place where the rest of the martyrs lie. There is a bird there that sits on top of the rocks and wears a face no bird has ever worn. Its voice is the voice of Dr. Cone. It folds the rocks and forest and shadows into a room that he is able to enter and leave at will. Its walls are maps for the journey he is about to take. Each one works in only one direction.

CONE UNEARTHED

There was a man inside Dr. Cone who spoke through his mouth and walked with his feet and touched with his hands. When Dr. Cone died the man continued to live. All he could see was the night. All he could touch were the walls of his container. Later, when the doctor's assistant began to shovel away the loose soil from the doctor's grave, he thought he heard a scratching noise coming from below. He assumed it was the rats and continued digging. The hand that pushed the lid open from the inside was familiar enough. But there would be no carnival exhibit made from this body. Even though it had started to decay it still continued to move.

CONE LECTURES

When Dr. Cone opened the capsule he did not like what he found. It was dark and green and swollen and seemed to have a life of its own. Before he could close the container, a little bit of it plopped onto the table and slithered quickly out of sight. Wherever it moved it left a trail of bubbly slime. The doctor searched for it in every corner of the laboratory but never saw it again. He was telling his apprentices about it when they all suddenly began to yawn and soon fell into a deep sleep. They dreamed, each one of them, that it was the creature itself, having assumed the appearance of Dr. Cone, that now lectured them. That was why they were not surprised when the door behind them resounded with a loud and chilling knock. When they opened it, they found what appeared to be the real doctor, gasping madly out of breath. They brought him inside, and were about to wrap him in his ceremonial garment, when a sharp noise roused them from their collective dream. Before them stood Dr. Cone, tapping his wand, waiting for any one of them at all to answer his sincere and most pointed question.

CONE CROSSES

Dr. Cone crossed the same river again and again. Each current and eddy, each fish and plant and rock, each insect and turtle, was exactly the same, and in exactly the same place, each time he crossed. But it was a different Dr. Cone who crossed each time. He was never the same. Sometimes he had an extra arm or a weirdly shaped head or a different kind of appendage he could not identify. Sometimes he was happy or sad or filled with dark thoughts or unfamiliar emotions. He changed and continued to change each time he stepped into the river that was always the same.

THE DARK ARK

The dark ark followed the other ark just out of sight. It contained only those creatures which god did not want to save. There was one of each. The dragon and the satyr and the unicorn and the griffin and all the others seemed to get along remarkably well. As the waters continued to rise, god's chosen captain steered the craft carefully through the rising swells. At first the doctor had hesitated to take control of the vessel, but he soon realized it was an offer that he could not refuse. He even stopped questioning why he was the one who was chosen. The troll was asking yet another question about the sea when the doctor first noticed that the sky was beginning to clear. He kept on sailing as the waters started to recede. Up ahead he could just make out the outline of the first ark, which had come to rest on top of a barely visible peak. But he continued to sail on. Eventually the waters dropped back to their normal level, but still the doctor could not find the right place to land his vessel. He knew there was only one thing he could do. He lay down on the deck and willed himself into a deep sleep. When he awoke on the dream ark, he visited all of the creatures in their dreams and invited them to join him there. Months later, when the captain of the first ark found the dark ark washed on shore, there were no living creatures on board. The doctor had kept them all inside his dream, so that they could visit the new generations whenever they were needed. That is why we still know them today.

THE WERE-BALLERINA

When the moon was full the were-ballerina changed into Dr. Cone. He had no knowledge of what he had been before. He remembered only his experiments, the wonderful marvelous experiments that allowed him to extend his mind from the cold wastelands of the deep mountains to the dense and puzzling jungles where the ancient rivers grew. There he had spoken with the animals and gathered information no man had ever known. He thought it had changed him, but he wasn't sure how. He felt stronger, yet more sensitized, than he had ever been before. Yet he knew that something was missing. When he changed again, the were-ballerina danced as she had never danced before, telling the stories of animals filled with hidden knowledge that they almost never shared.

CONE EMPLOYED

Dr. Cone sharpens the blade on the machine. He wants to work swiftly. He knows all eyes will be upon him as he stands on the platform, his identity hidden behind the frayed hood he inherited from his father. This would be his first time on center stage, his victim known to all as the king's mistress, and to himself, as his mother.

THE ELVES

The elves got tired of making shoes in the night while Dr. Cone slept. They decided to become barbers instead. Each night they snuck out of the laboratory and crept into windows around the village, trimming the hair of the sleeping inhabitants into weird and discomforting shapes. The doctor never realized what they were doing since one or two always stayed behind to continue making the shoes that paid for the running of the laboratory. But eventually the elves were seen, first by a tardy lamplighter, and then by the dairyman whose cart was too full to climb the steep incline of Half Moon Street. Rumors of their activities spread quickly through the town, and soon the doctor reluctantly opened his loudly pounding door to find hundreds of villagers with torches and pitchforks, yelling loudly and pointing at their strangely cut hair. The elves, of course, were never seen again. They had disappeared into the catacombs as soon as they heard the town folk at the door. Soon they were at sea in a boat they had secreted away years before for just such an occasion. But they were not forgotten. Long after the villagers had dispatched the good doctor from their lives, rumors still continued to reach them about elves in Prague and Venice and Dubrovnik who crept out each night, giving unusual haircuts to those who rested too deeply in their dreams to notice.

CONE RANTS

Dr. Cone is ranting to the rabbits. He wants them to know the truth. They are reluctant at first, but soon most of them start to think correctly. They quickly learn even the most subtle points of doctrine and are soon writing their own manifestos of belief and transformation. Once the doctor approves their texts, he sends them on their way to spread his teachings into even the most distant burrows. Only the white one remains. It has proved to be a most difficult case. It keeps looking at its watch as if it needed to be someplace else. But the doctor doesn't give up. Over and over again he explains the simplest tenets of doctrine to the white one, but somehow it just doesn't get it. It always seems distracted by something. The doctor sighs and turns his back on the rabbit for a moment to gather his thoughts, but when he turns again he sees it hopping quickly away, down into the valley where a young girl is enjoying a solitary picnic. The doctor shakes his head. He knows the rabbit will come to a bad end once the revolution opens its magnificent bloom.

Acknowledgments

The pieces included here were written between 1985 and 2009. They were previously collected in *Cone Investigates* (Poets Wear Prada, 2007, 2009) and *Cone Unearthed* (a private edition published in 2014 to celebrate a reading by the author at the Green Pavilion). Three of the episodes were also reprinted in the issue titled *True Adventures* of the author's private letter.

Thanks to the editors who previously published some of the individual episodes:

"Cone Travels":   *Artful Dodge, Stained Sheets*

"Cone Investigates": *Artful Dodge*

"Cone Transformed":   *Artful Dodge*

"Cone Martyred":   *Skidrow Penthouse*

"The Dark Ark":   *Skidrow Penthouse*

"The Elves":   *Brownstone Poets 2017 Anthology*

"Cone Rants":   *White Rabbit*

The cover collage first appeared in *Otoliths*.

Thanks to Roxanne Hoffman, who more than anyone else helped Dr. Cone step into the visible world.

About the Author

Bob Heman has been writing prose poems regularly for over forty years. Besides his Dr. Cone pieces, his prose poems include "The Serpent Variations," a long series that bounces off of the legends of the serpent and the garden; "Lore," a short series inspired mostly by fairy tales; "Footnotes For the Future," a series written using an experimental process [collected in 2019 in *The House of Grand Farewells*, published by Luna Bisonte Prods]; and his ongoing "Information" series.

His prose poems have appeared in numerous journals, including *Sentence, The Prose Poem: An International Journal, Caliban, Otoliths, Paragraph, Quick Fiction, Hanging Loose, Artful Dodge, Skidrow Penthouse,* and *First Intensity.* They are included in the anthologies *A Cast-Iron Aeroplane That Can Actually Fly: Commentaries from 80 Contemporary American Poets on Their Prose Poetry* (MadHat Press), *An Introduction to the Prose Poem* (Firewheel Editions), and *The Best of the Prose Poem: An International Journal* (White Pine Press). His collections *How It All Began* and *Demographics, or, The Hats They Are Allowed to Wear* are available as free downloads from Quale Press.

During the late 1970s he was artist-in-residence at the Brooklyn Museum. His collages, drawings, and "participatory cut-out multiples on paper" have been featured in a small two-man show at the Museum and included in group shows in Brooklyn, New York, Los Angeles, and Toronto. A one-man retrospective of his "cut-outs" was shown in 1979 at the Downtown

Cultural Center, an exhibition and performance space operated by BACA, the Brooklyn Arts and Cultural Association (now known as Brooklyn Arts Council, or BAC).

Since 1971, Bob Heman has edited *CLWN WR*, formerly *Clown War*, one of 84 "important magazines" honored with annotation in *The Little Magazine in America: A Modern Documentary History* (Pushcart Press, 1978). Among its special issues were Ted Berrigan's *Carrying a Torch*, F.A. Nettelbeck's *Bar Napkin Poems*, and the *Selected Prose Poems* of Belgian Surrealist Paul Colinet.

He has lived in Brooklyn for most of his adult life.

Selected Other Works by Bob Heman

The Number 5 Is Always Suspect
(with Cindy Hochman)
Rockford, MI: Presa Press, 2019.

The House of Grand Farewells
Columbus, OH: Luna Bisonte Prods, 2019.

As If
Brooklyn: privately printed, 2018.

Acts of Innuendo
Brooklyn: privately printed, 2016.

as much as you think you know
Brooklyn: privately printed, 2014.

[26 Structures]
Brooklyn: privately printed, 2010.

Demographics, or, The Hats They Are Allowed to Wear
N.p.: Quale Press, 2009.

Recent Information
New Orleans: Fell Swoop, 2007.

How It All Began
N.p.: Quale Press, 2007.

ABOUT THE TYPE & DECORATIONS

Text for this book is set in Book Antiqua, designed after Hermann Zapf's Palatino (Stempel Type Foundry, 1949) by the Monotype Type Drawing Office for Microsoft and released in 1991. A custom version of Book Antiqua was subsequently developed by Monotype as a corporate font for the Parliament of the United Kingdom. We've chosen it here, to paraphrase poet and freelance writer Adrienne Raphael, because surrealist time travel could only be in Book Antiqua. ["The Font of Poetry, the Poetry of Font," *The Paris Review*, August 3, 2015, accessed November 12, 2017, https://www.theparisreview.org/blog/2015/08/03/the-font-of-poetry-the-poetry-of-font/]

The border of the *schmutztitel* is a digital reproduction of an ornately engraved architectural frame from the first of 19 plates, illustrating distillation and other alchemical processes, bound at the end of *Dell'elixir vitae* [On the Elixir of Life] by Donato d'Eremita, published in Naples by Secondino Roncagliolo in 1624, and now held in the Alchemy Collection of the Getty Research Institute. [*The Internet Archive*, September 20, 2010, accessed November 9, 2017, https://archive.org/details/dellelixirvitae00dona]

The mythic map border used for the Table of Contents is the editor's distillation of a lost image of unknown source.

www.ingramcontent.com/pod-product-compliance
Lightning Source LLC
Chambersburg PA
CBHW031904170626
46807CB00004B/1897